Watch out! Big Bro's Coming!

D1343986

For Graham,
Katy and Lauren

First published 1997 by Walker Books Ltd
87 Vauxhall Walk, London SE11 5HJ
This edition published 2012
2 4 6 8 10 9 7 5 3 1
© 1997 Jez Alborough
The right of Jez Alborough to be identified
as author/illustrator of this work has been
asserted by him in accordance with the
Copyright, Designs and Patents Act 1988
This book has been typeset in
ITC Usherwood
Printed in China
British Library Cataloguing
in Publication Data:
a catalogue record for this book is
available from the British Library
ISBN 978-1-4063-3445-6
www.walker.co.uk

Watch out! Big Bro's coming!

Jez Alborough

WALKER BOOKS
AND SUBSIDIARIES

LONDON · BOSTON · SYDNEY · AUCKLAND

"Help!" squeaked a mouse.
"He's coming!"

"Who's coming?" asked a frog.

"Big Bro," said the mouse.
"He's rough, he's tough,
and he's big."

"Big?" said the frog. "How big?"

The mouse stretched out his arms as wide as they could go. "This big," he cried, and he scampered off to hide.

"Look out!" croaked the frog.
"Big Bro's coming!"

"Big who?" asked the parrot.

"Big Bro," said the frog. "He's rough,
he's tough, and he's really big."

"Really big?" said the parrot. "How big?"

The frog
stretched out
his arms as wide
as they could go.
"This big," he cried,
and he hopped off to hide.

"Watch out!" squawked the parrot.
"Big Bro's coming!"

"Who's he?" asked
the chimpanzee.

"Don't you know Big Bro?"
asked the parrot.
"He's rough, he's tough,
and he's ever so big."

"Ever so big?" said the
chimpanzee. "How big?"

The parrot stretched out his wings
as wide as they could go.
"This big," he cried,
and he flapped off
to hide.

"Ooh-ooh! Look out!"
whooped the chimpanzee.
"Big Bro's coming!"

"Big Joe?" said the elephant.

"No," said the chimpanzee.
"Big Bro. He's rough, he's tough,
and everybody knows how big
Big Bro is."

The elephant shook his head.
"I don't," he said.

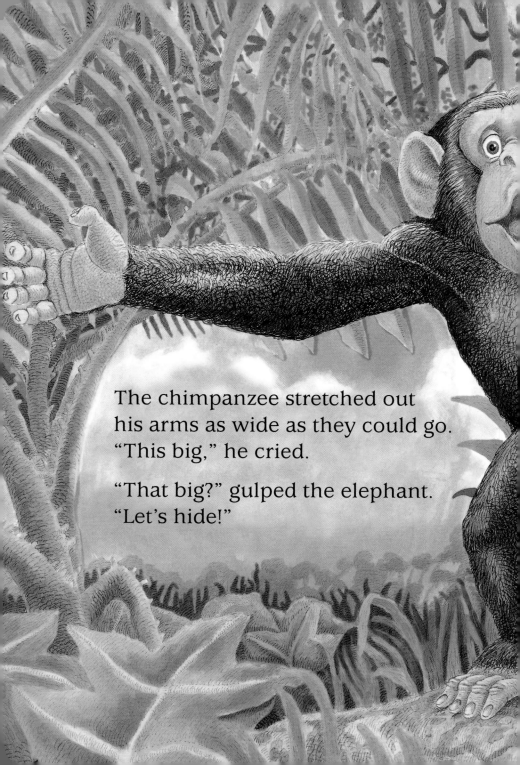

The chimpanzee stretched out his arms as wide as they could go. "This big," he cried.

"That big?" gulped the elephant. "Let's hide!"

So there they all were,
hiding and waiting,
waiting and hiding.

"Where is he?" asked
the elephant.

"Shhh," said the chimpanzee.
"I don't know."

"Why don't you creep out
and have a look around?"
whispered the elephant.

"Not me," said the chimpanzee.

"Not me," said the parrot.

"Not me," said the frog.

"All right," said the mouse. "As you're all so frightened, I'll go."

The mouse tiptoed ever so slowly out from his hiding place.

He looked this way and that way to see if he could see Big Bro.

And then…

"He's coming!"
shrieked the mouse.

"H …

    h …

      h …

        hide!"

Big Bro came closer and closer and closer. Everyone covered their eyes.

"Oh no," whispered the frog.

"Help," gasped the parrot.

"I can hear something coming," whined the chimpanzee.

"It's him," whimpered the elephant. *"It's ... it's ..."*

"BIG BRO!"

shrieked the mouse.

"Is that Big Bro?" asked
the frog.

"He's tiny," said the parrot.

"Teeny weeny,"
said the chimpanzee.

"He's a mouse,"
said the elephant.

Big Bro looked up
at them all, took a
deep breath,
and said …

"Come on, Little Bro,"
said Big Bro. "Mum wants
you back home *now*!"

"Wow," said the elephant.

"Phew," said the chimpanzee.

"He is rough," said the parrot.

"And tough," said the frog.

BIG!"

Titles in this series

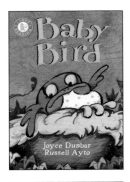 Baby Bird
Joyce Dunbar
Russell Ayto

 Michael Rosen
Little Rabbit Foo Foo
Arthur Robins

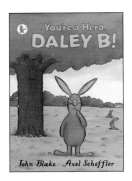 You're a Hero
DALEY B!
John Blake   Axel Scheffler

 "Go tell it to the toucan!"
Colin West

 I Don't Like Gloria!
Kaye Umansky
Margaret Chamberlain

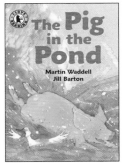 The Pig in the Pond
Martin Waddell
Jill Barton

 Jez Alborough
Watch out! Big Bro's coming!

 Polly Dunbar
PENGUIN

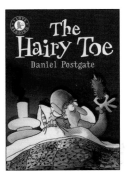 The Hairy Toe
Daniel Postgate

 Leon and Bob
SIMON JAMES

Available
from all good
booksellers

 www.walker.co.uk